To the memory of our wonderful cat Tex
and my mother-in-law's goldfish

American edition published in 2012 by Andersen Press USA,
an imprint of Andersen Press Ltd.
www.andersenpressusa.com

First published in Great Britain in 2012 by Andersen Press Ltd.,
20 Vauxhall Bridge Road, London SW1V 2SA.
Published in Australia by Random House Australia Pty.,
Level 3, 100 Pacific Highway, North Sydney, NSW 2060.
Text and illustrations copyright © Michael Foreman, 2012

Distributed in the United States and Canada
by Lerner Publishing Group, Inc.
241 First Avenue North Minneapolis, MN 55401 U.S.A.
www.lernerbooks.com

Color separated in Switzerland by Photolitho AG, Zürich.
Printed and bound in Singapore by Tien Wah Press.
Michael Foreman has used watercolors in this book.

Library of Congress Cataloging in Publication Data available.
ISBN: 978–1–4677–0317–8

1 – TWP – 3/7/12
This book has been printed on acid-free paper.

FRIENDS

MICHAEL FOREMAN

ANDERSEN PRESS USA

I'm lucky.
I'm a cat.
I can wander wild and free,
far and wide.

Poor old Bubble.
He's a fish . . .
Stuck in his tank.

He swims round and round,
down to the bottom, up to the top.
Then he swims round and round the other way.

Then he just looks at me and sighs.
He is my friend. He breaks my heart.

One day, when I was wandering wild and free,
I had a thought . . .

The bucket gave me an idea.

"Come on, Bubble. Jump!"

"Well done!"

I took Bubble to the pond in the park.
His eyes grew big and round.

He sighed and marveled at the ducks and flying geese,
and the shadowy fish swimming among the water lilies.
He sighed . . .

"You've seen nothing yet," I said.

Then I took him to the river. His eyes grew even bigger. He had never seen so much water!

Then we followed the river to the wide, wide sea.

We watched the waves rolling in from the horizon
and the schools of fish swimming in the dark depths.

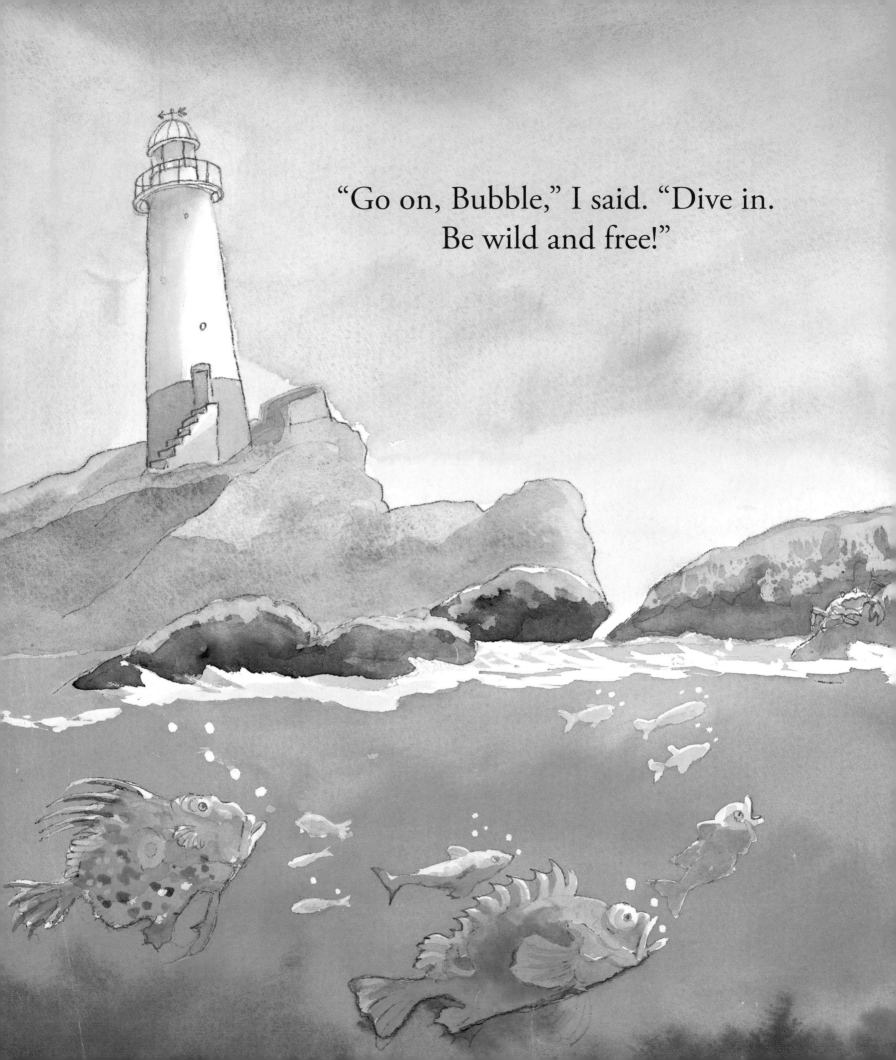

"Go on, Bubble," I said. "Dive in.
Be wild and free!"

But he looked at me and this time he didn't sigh.
He shook his head . . . and smiled a bubbly smile.
"Let's go home," he said.
"There may be lots of other fish in the sea,
but I might never find a friend like you."

So now we wander wild and free,
together, to the pond, the river, and the sea.

Sometimes we wander the hills and
woods above the city . . .

and, on wet days, we explore
the great city itself.

Bubble and me
Have a world to see
From here . . .

MOUSA LISA

Edouard Decat

. . . to the rainbow's end.